William Patterson Jones

The myth of Stone Idol

A love legend of Dakota

William Patterson Jones

The myth of Stone Idol
A love legend of Dakota

ISBN/EAN: 9783337150068

Printed in Europe, USA, Canada, Australia, Japan

Cover: Foto ©Andreas Hilbeck / pixelio.de

More available books at **www.hansebooks.com**

THE MYTH OF STONE IDOL.

A LOVE LEGEND OF DAKOTA.

BY

WILLIAM P. JONES, A. M.,

LATE PRESIDENT OF THE NORTHWESTERN FEMALE COLLEGE,
EVANSTON, ILL.

CHICAGO:
S. C. GRIGGS AND COMPANY.
1876.

TO HER,

WHO HAS ILLUSTRATED

WOMANLY FAITHFULNESS AND DEVOTION,

AS NO POET'S VERSE OR GRAVER'S BURIN

COULD EVER DO,

THIS SIMPLE SONG IS

AFFECTIONATELY INSCRIBED.

PREFACE.

I T is an echo of one of those fast-expiring songs
of the wilderness, which, only a few years ago,
filled all this grand western world with poetry.
It is a simple song, but the untutored Æolian sounding
in some splintered forest bough has found a well-pleased
listener, and so, perchance, may this.

How often have I sat in the pilot-house, or on the
deck of the good old-time Mississippi steamers, when
river and island and darkly-wooded shores, wrapt in
the weird moonlight, seemed a ghost realm; — when
the breath of the throbbing engines streamed over us
and far out into the night in spark and flame-lit
banners of snowy steam and pitch-black smoke, whose
wild reflections on the angry waters in the vessel's
wake glared like a troop of pursuing demons; and

then, when every nerve was excited to utmost tensity, listened with boyish delight to the pilots and fur-traders reciting the thrilling legends of our rivers and our prairies!

Not seldom, too, have I sought out the early settlers and the Indians themselves, and gathered the wild clusters of olden story, full of the racy wine of the wilderness, fresh from their own lips.

But many a time has a feeling of sadness mingled with my listening pleasure at thought, that, for want of chroniclers, these charming lyrics and heroics must be lost to the hereafter; that these many-colored leaves of the Indian autumn, which should be pressed between golden covers and preserved to adorn our libraries, seemed all destined to an early burial under the snows of that eternal winter which must soon bring oblivion to the last of the Aborigines.

The themes of these legends are as various as the passions of the human heart. The life of the wilderness stands all revealed in them: its deathless friendships and loves, and its deadly hates and cruelties; its heroics of fidelity and its infamies of treachery. Yes, the cardinal passions — (best proof of the unity of mankind) — with their gleamings of sunshine and flashes of lightning rifting the darkness, which but for them would have been oblivion long ago, are all at play here, filling our woods and prairies with drama and tragedy. And *"Le Grand Passion"* of the world of homes and palaces is the grand passion here also.

If any one charges the following verses with an excess of tender sentiment, let him remember, that, in a state of nature, love and imagination are as unrestrained of growth as hate and revenge; and let the many still surviving legends of the tribes attest that no more extravagant love-romances have ever been sung than are recited around Indian camp fires. Every prominent river-bluff and precipice and cavern and lake and waterfall once had its story of love's fruition or suffering and devotion. Here it was a wooing and mating, there a heart-breaking and suicide. Why all this, if the Indian, except when excited by the lower appetites and passions, is all stolidity?

The subject of this little poem was furnished years ago in a few lines of the journal of Lewis and Clark's famous expedition to the head-waters of the Missouri and Columbia rivers, in 1804–5, published by order of Congress. Much of the material, however, has been drawn from other sources, oral and written; some of which are referred to in the notes at the close of the book, for which a careful reading is bespoken.

Do I hear the public whispering, "What made him do it?" What, but only this;—to show yet once again that the theme which never gets stale, the story that never grows old, is the same in all lands, and among all peoples, *love faithful until death*, aureole of the universal sainthood.

PRELUDE.

LOVE, only, is the universal god.

    Whether enthroned as Deity above

Or meekly serving on earth's humble sod,

    Enshrined in man, a worshiped human love,

All nations bow to it and call it lord.

The sole Life-Essence! everywhere adored.

THE MYTH OF STONE IDOL.

OU have heard it,—the pretty romance of
Stone Idol?
How Indian maids, ere they robe for the bridal,
Send thither for flowers?
How maidens unwooed plant the buds in their tresses,
And lover to loved one his passion confesses
With a sprig from its bowers?

How the maiden beloved, its full meaning divining,
If she take it, the blooms in her braidings entwining,
Wears a pledge of affiance?
And an oath by Stone Idol, that lover will never
Prove false to his true love, but love her forever,
Wins the firmest reliance.

So woman ne'er passes that way but she turneth,
Plucks some sprig near the rock and a sacrifice burneth
    'Neath this monument hoary.
'Tis a popular faith — this quaint superstition —
Would you learn how it sprang from an ancient
    tradition ?
        Then list to the story.

'Twas where Missouri's waters flow
    Through prairies of enameled green,
That stretch from sunset's peaks of snow
    To Mississippi's crystal sheen ;
Where still the Indian hunters rove
    O'er boundless plains from woodlands free,
Save here and there a' lovely grove
    Set like an islet in the sea,
Where all is beauty yet, and wild,
Unwasted by the pale-faced child ;

In region such, long moons ago,
As countless as the shells that strew
The shores Missouri's waters lave,
There lived a tribe of warriors brave.

The years, with their resistless tide,
Have swept this valiant band away;[1]
Yet not with them their memory died;
Their fame hath not such swift decay;
Full many a legendary tale
Still holds aside oblivion's veil
And speaks to men of other days
Those ancient warriors' blame or praise,
Attested down the years unknown
By pictograph and rough-hewn stone,[2]
Whereon, in symbols rude, are read
The archives of a nation dead,
With bowlders, mounds and mountain-rents,
And river bluffs, for monuments.

As yet this gallant tribe was young,
    Though far and wide its fame had spread,
For stouter bow no warriors strung,
    In chase no hunters swifter sped;
Nor fairer, truer women smiled
Than wrought to bless those rovers wild;
Well pleased, for them to dress the fish,
The venison, and the savory dish
Of juicy bulbs and tender herbs,
Or fetch the drink from pebbly curbs;
To till the corn-ridge in the glade,
Or pluck and husk the green ears' blade
And roast it in the glowing ash,
Or mix the ambrosial succotash;
To raise for them the fragrant weed,
And dress and sew the fur, and bead
The wampum and the moccasin;
    Or strike and pitch the shifting tent,

And fill the magic ring within
　　With children's witching merriment.

Fit scion of such race was he,
Who, with his faithful maid, shall be
The burden of our minstrelsy.

CANTO I.

-

THE WOOING.

THE glorious prairies of the West!
  Whoe'er their verdant sod hath pressed
  Must feel how weak, how vain 'twould be,
  How almost like to mockery,
To venture, in a minstrel's lay,
Their matchless beauty to portray.
To-night such task were doubly vain,
For Indian summer haunts the plain,
(The "golden moons." that come again,
  When all their burning rage has set,
To smoke the calumet with men,
  And leave the earth with sad regret.)

Far rolls the plain on every hand
　　And seems a sea, with emerald waves,
Waves such as rise far out from land
　　When Zephyr in the ocean laves.
The river sweeps unruffled by;
Within the stars reflected lie,
And like a jeweled pavement seem
Beneath the swiftly current stream.
Midway the gipsy Moon doth float
In her silver, scalloped boat,
Nor lifteth oar to scull or steer,
As only fain to sit and hear
Those tinkling roundels, faint and low,
From song-lipped ripples far below.

　　Around yon bend that's just in sight,
On river bank bestrewn with flowers,
　　Dance scores of Indian braves to-night,
And sport away the moon-lit hours:

With wild, fantastic trip and spring'

E'er circling an enchanted ring

Of merry maidens' laughing eyes,—

Where *love* oft sits, in poor disguise,

Such times, in eager gaze and glee

Forgetting half its coquetry.

　　But hist! a sound the Zephyr bore!

It seemed the dipping of an oar.

Again! and yet nor far nor nigh

Doth living object greet the eye.

Perchance it was the plash — so like —

Of skipping perch, or darting pike,

Or basking water-snake, or frog,

Or turtle sliding from its log,

Or loosened turfs that seek the tide'

From crumbling, flood-washed river side.

Perchance! And yet, *there* seems to float,

A something, not unlike a boat.

Mayhap it is a lone canoe,

Which yon green isle has hid from view.

Nearer it comes, and nearer still,

Slow drifting at the current's will.

And now it *is* a boat, 'tis plain,

Nor drifts unbidden to the main,

But, like a thing of thought, doth bear

Its master and some partner fair.

What youthful brave and trusting maid

Do thus the merry dance evade,

And hither bent, in secret mood

Crave all their joy of solitude?

That manly form must surely be

The brave young warrior, Men-no-wee,

And she, the fair one of the twain,

Lel-lu-la, belle of all the plain.

Were prudish dames ne'er disobeyed,'

Nor clannish codes, no Indian maid

Were ever seen thus far away
From camp, or guardian watch and sway.
But Love is Love, where'er you find it,
And who, the wide world o'er, can bind it?
In frozen North, in East or West
   Or burning South, 'tis all the same,
   Who breathes the intoxicating flame
No longer vaunts the Stoic breast,
Nor bows to law or threatening sires,
But moves him as the sprite inspires:
And Honor hath no safer shield
Than true-love to his maid doth yield.

   So these have left the throng behind
And stolen down the stream to find
Some spot beyond all list'ners' ken,
Where they may interchange again
The sacred vows, the pledges dear,
They could not, when the crowd was near.

Now Men-no-wee has dropt the oar
And guides the light canoe no more,
Nor heeds he object far or nigh,
The dew-gemmed earth or star-gemmed sky;
His arm is round Lel-lu-la's waist,
His fingers through her soft hair laced,
And to his lip and to his eye
Her eye, *her* lip now make reply.
Then wherefore should he care for aught
Save her, the soul of every thought,
Save her, whose love-reflected face,
On darkest war-path, farthest chase,
Forever present to his heart,
Ne'er leaves him, though herself depart —
This actual self, this throbbing real,
Dear flesh and blood of his ideal,
That now leans fondly on his arm,
A living, life-absorbing charm.

Nay, let no common thought transgress
The borders of such happiness.
Where all seems lost to outward sense
There Love's true bound'ries just commence,
And he who thither wins his way
May bask in her ecstatic ray.
Such is the spiritual bound
Which these fond hearts this hour have
    found;
And now, abstract from all beside,
Their thoughts like streams commingling glide,
Which naught about them can divide.
Beneath their boat the waters play
And sing a fairy roundelay;
Above their heads the spangled sky
Rears its jeweled arches high;
The waving prairies far and nigh
'Neath a flood of glory lie;

And on the river margin, near,
Stands a spright and antlered deer,
Like a sentinel of love
Watching for their boat above.
But yet the maid and Men-no-wee
None of all these beauties see.

Thus, captive to a common spell,
Beloving, and beloved as well,
Each wholly slaved and wholly bound
Is happier than a monarch crowned,
Nor would exchange this moment's bliss
For thrice ten thousand worlds like this.
Young Men-no-wee is bending now
Above Lel-lu-la's orbéd brow;
His fingers dally with the meshes
Of the maiden's raven tresses;
He gazes in her ebon eyes,
In which such thrall of beauty lies;

He breathes her breath, like odored gales
Perfumed in full blown flower-vales;
Then tints her cheek and lips with kisses,
    And, raptured by the thrilling vein
    That ever prompts the amorous strain,
And Thought for Joy's wild steed dismisses,
Gives Passion free, abandoned rein
To gallop o'er Love's wordy plain.

MEN-NO-WEE.

Maid of the ardent, love-lit eye,
    Kindling my soul with rapture high,
Dark-eyed child of the prairies free,
How shall I utter my love for thee?
    All of the voices that speak in air,—
    Tones that the lips of the zephyrs bear,
Music of birds in their summer glee,
Chirping of cricket and humming of bee,

Babblings of rills as they skip on their way,

Tunes that the fountains and waterfalls play,

Hymns of the winds in their wild rejoice,

Anthems which swell in the thunder's voice,

Pipings of minstrels that woo the fair,—

All of them, breathed in one harmony rare,

Such, that when "Spirit Land" caught the strain

Souls of the blest would haste earthward again,

All of them could not my love declare.

Lel-lu-la lists with joy the while,

Delight imprinted in her smile,

Till, as the final word is said,

Her vermeiled cheek takes deeper red,

And, yielding to the witchery

Of maiden's sex-born coquetry,

Wherewith she shrewdly makes her lover

His passion's deepest depths discover,

Or to her thirsty heart repeat
The draught of love each time more sweet,
She turns away, and coyly tries
To veil her love in peevish guise;
A feigned reproof her lips divides,
And thus in pettish tone she chides:

LEL-LU-LA.

Full oft thou hast sung me this song, Men-no-wee,
O see'st thou not thou art wearying me?
Must maidens be list'ning forever to love?
Dost thou think we are all as the languishing dove,
That bird that is cooing its love-notes forever,
And alters the theme of its minstrelsy never?
Hast thou failed to observe how nature doth change
And vary the beauties amid which we range?
The sky wears not always the same azure hue,
The earth does not always lie glist'ning in dew,

The colors of sunset are never the same
For an eve or an instant — so never grow tame;
The bud of the rose keeps not always unblown,
But opes, that its lovelier tints may be shown;
Then wherefore do lovers ne'er vary their strain,
But sing us the same song again and again?

MEN-NO-WEE.

Maiden with dallying tresses dight,
Tresses as dark as the plumes of night,
Child of the prairies, mischanced in birth,
Meant but for "Spirit Land," strayed to the earth,
So hath thy beauty enslaved my heart,
Never would I from thy presence depart
All of the treasures that 'neath us lie,
All of the stars that adorn the sky,
All of the riches on land and sea
Could not entice me to stray from thee.

LEL-LU-LA.

O fie, Men-no-wee, wilt thou never give o'er?
'Tis the very same song thou wast singing before,
And why would'st thou weary my life with this tale
Which thou seemest to think cannot ever grow stale?
O change thy theme now, and sing of the flowers;
The fawns in the valley; the birds in their bowers;
Of yon bright eyes of heaven which look on us now;
Of this balm-laden breeze that is kissing my brow.
Can'st thou solve me the myst'ry, whence, wherefore
    they blow
Or sparkle or flourish? 'Twere pleasant to know.

MEN-NO-WEE.

Joy of my soul and my being's light!
  Lu-la, fair as the sunbeam bright,
Matchless in feature and symmetry,
How shall I sing of aught else than thee?

Beauty on earth and beauty in sky,
　　Serve but to image thy charms to my eye,
Image them *fadingly,* even as now
Waters beneath us do mirror thy brow.
　　Flowers, by tintings and rich perfumes,
　　Birds, by their carols and brilliant plumes,
Fawns, by their grace in each motion and limb,
Stars, by their lustre, no age can dim,
　　Winds, by their breathings of fragrance and song,
　　All that is lovely, by sympathy strong,
Calls to my mind some perfection of thine,
Prompts me to worship, with thee for my shrine.

LEL-LU-LA.

O stay, Men-no-wee, thou can'st tell me no more!
Thou'st uttered thy soul, and my heart runneth o'er;
Then rest, and as I have been list'ning to thee,
So now be thou patient, and hearken to me.

SONG.

The warrior has his bow and shield,
    His battle-axe and spear,
But woman's all in all is love,
    Her only strength and cheer.

The hunter has his bounding steed,
    His quiver, dart and knife,
But woman's all in all is love,
    The chase of all her life.

Her lord, for pleasure or for fame,
    O'er all the earth may roam,
But woman's all in all is love,
    And where that is, is home.

Thou'rt brave as valor's self, my love,
    And should'st not thou be true?

Truth, valor, honor are but one,
    So thou and falsehood two.

Thou bring'st me love, with pledge of truth,
    To doubt thee were to die;
Henceforth thou art my all in all,
    And where thou art, am I.

    The song is done, the strain is o'er,
    The music dies along the shore;
    The last faint echoes faintly roll,
    Like fading memories o'er the soul.
    Locked in one long and fond caress
    Of mutual love and tenderness,
    With feelings wrapt, as in a trance,
    And far too full for utterance,
    The lovers sit, nor heed how fly
    The lightning pinioned moments by,

Till on the green horizon's brim
The sinking moon grows quickly dim
And warns them by its waning light
How very far hath sped the night.
Now thinking of the homeward course
They turn to stem the current's force.
Good Men-no-wee, with native sleight,
Directs and speeds the boat aright,
While fair Lel-lu-la cheers the time
With sonnets quaint of Indian rhyme.
Thus, slowly, homeward tend the twain,
And Solitude resumes her reign.

CANTO II.

—

THE INTERDICTION.

AGAIN 'tis night, and, like the last,
  A night in beauty unsurpassed;
   A night that makes us feel the power
  Of placid moonlight's tranquil hour,
That mystic power, which thrills the breast,
While yet we know not why we're blest.

We wander, as we did before,
Along the wild Missouri's shore;
The same enrapturing beauties spread
Around, beneath and overhead:
While, to enrich the lovely view,
A mimic grove, of greenest hue,

Stands waving 'gainst the impending skies,
And in its quiet border lies
An Indian village, still and fair
As if 'twere only painted there.
There dwells Shee-wau amid his braves
Like some tall elm, that towering waves
Its regal branches over all
The forest lords which 'neath it fall.
Yon stately wigwam's birchen dome
Makes all the chieftain's court and home.
There lies he now, at hour for rest,
Expecting midnight's wonted guest.
Never before in many a year
Has sleep refused to meet him here;
Not e'en when war its horrors wrought,
And prowling foes his slumbers sought;
When dread of midnight massacre
Filled every weaker heart with fear,

Nor when the tempest's crashing thunder
Seemed bursting heaven and earth asunder.
Oft has it been his lot to lie
With nothing o'er him but the sky;
Ofttimes the snow has been his bed,
With moss-grown log to rest his head,
Yet thus exposed he soundly slept
While beasts of prey about him crept,—
Unwakened by the bear's hoarse growl,
Unstartled by the wolf's fierce howl.

To-night all things seem wooing rest;
The softest furs his limbs invest.
An otter robe is o'er him spread,
A fawn-skin pillow props his head,
The open door admits the light
And fragrant breezes of the night
To dally with his hoary hairs
And lull him with Æolian airs;

Yet faithful sleep forsakes him now,
And leaves unsmoothed his wrinkled brow.
Why does the chieftain restless lie?
Why comes not slumber to his eye?
What present care affects him more
Than all life's gathered ills before?

Ah! sorely is his soul oppressed,
For she, of all life's gifts the best,
Lies anguished now in heart and brain
By poison Fate hath made her drain
From lips that fain would yield their breath,
Could that but meet the stern demand
Of law's inflexible command,
Which now seems working double death.

Lel-lu-la is his only child;
Of seven that once about him smiled

The one lone joy that Fate has left:
For three, e'en from his side, were cleft
By battle's bloody axe, and three,—
    O Hate, and Vengeance, never! never!
    Forget that deed,—'tis damned forever!—
Were massacred most fiendishly!
Mother and babes and wife asleep
At night,—at morn a bloody heap!

    Then surely 'tis not strange that she,
The sole sprout of that parent tree,
Should be his being's prop and pride,
Nor e'er know wish that he denied
Till now:—yes, now! 'Tis Fate's decree
    That all must taste the bitter tree
    Of trial and adversity,
And now, poor child, it fruits for thee.

¹To-night, ere Twilight left the West
And Day had drawn his tent, to rest,
He strode the lodge with troubled air,
Nor touched the evening's smoking fare,
Nor spoke, but motioned from his sight
The wondering menials,⁷ mute with fright,
Then laid away his pipe, untried,
And called the maiden to his side.

  Nor waited she, but instant flew
To chase those fright'ning clouds apace,
    Around his neck her warm arms threw
And laid her cheek against his face.

    To weep for torture's cruel pang,
Or death, or sting of hunger's fang,
Or aught that mortal ill can do,
Would ne'er become a warrior true;
Yet doubt not Love can sometimes thaw
The veriest stone of flesh, and draw

The sternest Indian's soul to bring
A tribute tear, Death could not wring.

So fared the iron chief, Shee-wan,
That time he felt those dear arms draw
Their filial clasp about his neck,
Starting a tear he could not check;
Since for such love his harsh return
Must be a mandate which should burn
Upon her brain like torturing fire:
And what to this, for doting sire,
Were foe's hot dart or flaming pyre?
This but his crackling flesh could scorch,
That to his soul applies the torch.

That single tear appalled her more
Than all the frowns he ever wore,
And, trembling with an unknown fear,
Nearer she pressed, and still more near,

As sparrow 'neath its parent's wing,
Making his breast her covering.

But soon, the traitor tear dismissed,
The terror from her brow was kissed
And thus he spoke:

"Lel-lu-la, child,
Fear not this passion, strangely wild —
An instant stronger than my strength —
'Tis conquered now, and thou at length
Shalt learn its cause, — how love for thee
And wish to spare thee misery
Have even wrung a tear from me.
Thou wilt not doubt my fondness then;
Nay! though I say that ne'er again
Those eyes must look on Men-no-wee
As else than foe to thee and me.

I deemed him once a warrior brave,

And worthy of the love we gave,

A lover of his tribe and chief,

Who ne'er would give a foe relief

Or freely spare the lives of those

For whom our deadliest hatred glows.

"Thou know'st what time the Mandans came,

Enwrapt our homes" in midnight flame

And massacred thy sleeping dame?

What time they scalped thy brothers twain?

And thy fair sister-babe was slain?

That time we called our scattered bands

Around those lodges' smouldering brands,

Around those loved ones' whitened bones,

And swore, by all thy nation owns

Of Powers in clouds and earth and hell,

That, till the last doomed Mandan fell,

His blood through palms of vengeance wrung,
Our bows should never go unstrung,
Our knives be sheathed, or hatchets laid
Or buried 'neath the Peace tree's shade:
We swore nor old nor young to spare,
Mother, nor babe, nor maiden fair,
But whelm the whole accursed brood
In one unpitying doom of blood.

" My child! my child! it must be so!
The oath must live! Who breaks it,—woe!
And yet, to-day, this Men-no-wee
Has spurned its fearful sanctity:
For straggling in the distant chase,
He chanced, in wild, secluded place,
Upon a Mandan, almost dead
From loss of blood, (right nobly shed
'Tis true! for near him, in his lair,
Lay slain a monstrous grizzly-bear.)

" Young Men-no-wee should then have done
The work of death so well begun;
But nay! he gave him drink, then bound
And gently stanched each bleeding wound,
And when he saw his foe revive ·
Turned *girl*, and bade him go alive!
For this, by all our ancient law,
And by the honor of Shee-wau,
He stands condemned his spear to yield,'
And toil his lifetime in the field.
Thus sore disgraced he ne'er can be
A lord to thee, a son to me.
So now thou must his love forego,
And he at morn his doom shall know."

Lel-lu-la heard; she raised no cry,
She did not weep nor make reply;
But stood as one of life bereft,

The death-pangs in her features left,—
A type of speechless agony,
The embodiment of misery.

O, strong and terrible is grief
When tears come not to give relief!
The stream that trickles through the mountain
Unpent, flows harmless from its fountain,
But bound, it bursts the solid rock,
And rends the mount with dreadful shock:
So griefs that weep slight wound impart,
But tears confined will burst the heart.

The chieftain did not see or hear
That woe too deep for word or tear;
Too dimly there the moonbeams shone
To make those lines of sorrow known,

And thence faint hope his fancy drew
That Time would soon Love's spell undo,
And heal that instant's cruel wound.
Yet feared he silence so profound,
And when anon a smothered moan
Escaped her heart, it seemed his own
Were melting into molten lead,
And half he wished his words unsaid!
Yet felt to yield were sore disgrace,
So, still resolved, with fond embrace
He strove to make her feel some part
Of parent love that wrung his heart:
Then blessed her for obedience past
And prayed her, while his life should last,
Ne'er give her sire cause for shame;
But, like her fearless, high-born dame,
Who never blanched for fear, or fled
From toil or pain, when Duty led,

Be stanch to brave the sternest doom.
"Go, child!" he cried, "dismiss this gloom!
Be in the bow of Destiny
    A flinted arrow! armed to go
At every mark that's set for thee;
    Nor bend at pain, nor glance from woe."

    On mats of flags and osier made
The richest Indian furs are laid,
Adorned with painted birds and flowers,
With pictured fruits and vines and bowers;
Embroidered with the choicest shells,
And scented with the sweetest smells
From camomile and rose fresh blown,
Which every morn are o'er them strewn.

    There lies Lel-lu-la now, unblest
By all these blandishments of rest,

A writhing sufferer,—a prey
To thoughts that gnaw her heart away.
Her breast is torn with inward pain;
A seething fever scalds her brain;
She sinks beneath her crushing fate,
By Love and Hope left desolate.

List, and catch the minstrelsy!
The air is stirred with melody.

SONG.

Awake, maiden, wake!
Sleep's rosy tendrils break!
O, leave thy beaver couch awhile
And haste to bless me with thy smile.
Awake, maiden, wake!
The air is balmy sweet to-night,
The earth with glist'ning dew is bright,

And like the love-light in thine eye
Shines the star-light in the sky.
    Then wake, maiden, wake!
    Let love thy slumbers break!
O, bid night's wizard shadows flee
And leave the world to thee and me!
    Awake, maiden, wake!

    Awake, maiden, wake!
    Thy shell-decked" couch forsake!
O, come where loving hearts may blend
In mutual joys that ne'er should end.
    Awake, maiden, wake!
My boat is by the river shore,
And waits thee now, as oft before,
While Love, impatient, bids thee haste,
Nor let her priceless moments waste.
    Then wake, maiden, wake!

Come, let us pleasure take!
And hours that brought us former bliss
Shall all seem dull or blank to this,
 So wake, maiden, wake!

Along the encampment's grassy lanes
So sing the amorous youths, in strains[12]
That stir full many a maiden's breast
With dreamings sweeter far than rest.

Erst, when the voice of Men-no-wee
Joined in the moon-lit minstrelsy,
Lel-lu-la drank the love-thrilled air
Like wine the matrons blest prepare[13]
From nectared clusters only found
Amid the Happy Hunting Ground,
Though suffered sometimes thence to flow
And mingle with the air below.

But now, alas for Men-no-wee!
He knows too well his misery
To join that once delightful strain,
Now turned to mocking, torturing pain.

They've told him that his generous deed
Was watched by one of· Envy's breed,–
A rival for his love and fame,—
Whose spleen has slimed his honored name
And marred it with a strange disgrace
That life nor death can e'er efface.

His chiefs have asked him of his act,
Himself hath witnessed to its fact,—
For Honor, though it dares to die,
Dares not for more than life, to lie.
The deed confessed,—himself hath seen
Lips knit o'er teeth that gnashed between,
And brows that frowned with direst bode,
As stern old war-chiefs past him strode.

So now, prepared, he waits his doom;
Nor dreads swift entrance to the tomb,
But only fears some sterner fate.

Yet wherefore for his sentence wait?
His neighing charger paws the plain,
Well trained at call to bite the rein;
The prairies free before him lie:
Then why not mount his barb and fly?
"*Fly! Fly!*" Avaunt! That ne'er can be!
Its foeman from his tribe may flee,
But never! surely *never,* he!

CANTO III.

THE APOTHEOSIS.

NIGHT'S stars had faded from the view
 And morn, in buskins gemmed with dew,
  Had wide, with rosy fingers, drawn
The gold-hemmed tent-folds of the dawn.

Shee-wau had summoned Men-no-wee
To learn his bitter destiny.
He came; he heard: what need we more?
As warriors bear, so he then bore,
And let the throes which wrung his breast,
As then, so now, go unexpressed.

The hours drag on at leaden pace
While we, with saddened musings, trace
A stream which to Missouri brings
The tribute of a hundred springs.
Along its banks our way has led
To where three princely elm-trees wed
Their locking branches overhead,
And from their green tiaras throw
Cool shade on violet beds below.

This is a spot by memory
Made holy ground to Men-no-wee.
'Twas here that first, in passioned tone,
He made his fervid fondness known.
'Twas here, Lel-lu-la by his side,
He won her pledge to be his bride;
Where many a blessed moon since then
Has heard her grant that pledge again.

But now those trysting-days are fled,
The hope that thrilled him then is dead;
Yet, though his thoughts through midnight grope,
Though fell despair has buried hope,
Though crushed in all save thrice-nerved pain,
He seeks the cherished spot again.

But ah! what lava-torrents roll,
In burning currents, through his soul,
As hallowed objects meet his eyes,
And thoughts of other days arise!
With iron grip he clasps his brain
As though he feared 'twould rend in twain,
And cries, "O, will they come no more!
Those days when joy's full banks ran o'er,
And bliss flowed constant in the breast,
When love made every moment blest?
Never can they return! no, never!
My cheerless sentence holds forever!

Of love bereft, an abject slave,

I've naught to pray for but the grave.

Then come, my friendly blade, set free

This tortured slave of misery.

Yet nay! A voice within me cries:

'None but the veriest *coward* flies

To self-destruction! who denies

He *fears* to *suffer*—therefore dies!'

Nay! I can breast the fiercest fate,

But she, my idol desolate,

Must not such suffering crush her heart?

Or can she"—the unworthy part

Is spared, for ere it is expressed

Lel-lu-la falls upon his breast.

O Love and Hopeless Agony!

Dumb in your deep intensity,

Why are ye destined thus to meet

And claim on earth the self-same seat!

'Twere better Love should never be
Than thus blow coals for Agony.

Long time they sat in silence there,
Struck mute with suffering and despair.
At last her soul's choked fountains start,
And tears relieve Lel-lu-la's heart.
Then speech returns, and thus she pleads:

"Alas! alas, my Men-no-wee!
Art thou so changed by misery
That thou can'st not one word bestow
To cherish her who loves thee so?
O, mention but my name once more —
'Twill half my murdered peace restore.
'Twere sweet to know that at this hour
Love still retains her wonted power.

And if this boon thou should'st deny
My swollen heart must break and die."

Sadly the warrior lifts his eyes:
"Great Spirit! grant, grant *now*," he sighs,
"The boon of death she seems to fear,
Since love no more can bless us here.
'Twere better both should perish so
Than thus to live, divorced by woe:
'Twere better sojourn with the dead
Than thus survive when hope has fled."

"O pause! Thou lov'st me still, I feel!"
Lel-lu-la cries, "then pray for weal,
But crave not death, for though 'twould be
Most welcome, were I torn from thee,
Yet while my arms thy neck entwine,
And thy warm cheek is pressed to mine,

I still will hope, despite my fears,
That Fate reserves us brighter years.
Though now we grope in darkest night,
Unguided by one ray of light,
Yet somewhere in this clouded air
Dwells One who hears the sufferer's prayer.
Him let us earnestly implore
To grant us former bliss once more;
Or, if such boon must be denied,
If *life* and *love* henceforth *divide*,
Then pray that death, before we sever,
Crush both our life and woe together."

'Tis spoken, and the twain have knelt
To Him, whose majesty is felt
And mystic sovereignty adored
Alike by sage and savage horde.
To Him, in strains of suppliancy,
Ascends the prayer of Men-no-wee:

"Almighty Te-wa-rooh-teh," Spirit True!

To whom all life and power and praise are due,

Thine is the attribute, by all confessed,

To aid the needy, succor the distressed:

To Thee we come, in grief's extremity,

And on Thy footstool bow the suppliant knee.

O, from the bowers of 'Spirit Land' above,

Regard Thy children with a Father's love.

Lo, how the arrows of a cruel fate

Hang festering in the hearts so blest of late.

Avert the judgments of a law unjust,

Which treads Thy milder instincts in the dust.

As Thou didst prompt this heart to aid a foe,

Let not Thy prompting be our overthrow!

Bind up the wounds a cruel law has made!

Revive the hopes that in the dust are laid!

Unite the tender chords of joy once more,

And all their soul-filled harmony restore!

Erase remembered pangs of agony,
Give back the cup of Love's full ecstasy!
Or if request so great must be denied,
Then aught bestow, so it do not divide
These hearts so closely, fondly, firmly bound,
And with the living coils of being wound.

O, let not these be rudely cleft;
Let both be first of life bereft.
Yea! if our dust may mingle here,
Grow in the same flowers from year to year,
In the same bridal-wreaths be bound,
While, in the Happy Hunting Ground,
Ourselves, united ne'er to sever,
Shall drink the same sweet founts forever,
And never pangs of suffering know,
Nor taste the poisoned dregs of woe,
Hence, Life! and hail, Felicity!
O, thither speed us instantly!

Yea! Te-wa-rooh-teh, Spirit True!
Let earth's false visions fade from view,
Strike off our clogs of suffering clay
And let these captive selves away."

———————

Where knelt those lovers years ago
Two massive rocks the Indians show;
On which the fairest flowers spring
And vines the most luxurious cling,
Which bind the two as close together
As if 'twere meant they ne'er should sever.
These — says the Indian Legendry —
Are Lu-la and her Men-no-wee.

Upon the hero's rocky crest
The sunshine seems a smile's behest.

IIis faithful dog beside him stands.

    The grapes, which were their only food

    When wand'ring, tentless, in the wood,

In clusters fill Lel-lu-la's hands;

And from her sun-lit forehead brown

Benignity itself looks down.

    Often doth sculptor Nature form,

With chiseling frost and hammering storm,

Rocks into rugged shapes of men;[15]

    Then, as the ancient prophets tell,

    Indue them with mysterious spell,

To guard some sacred mount or glen.

And like to such are these, 'tis true,

But think not thus *these* wonders grew.

Nay! Te-wa-rooh tch, Nature's Sire,

    In starry wigwam of the sky,

Heard his sad children's plaintive cry,
And granted all their souls' desire.

Long time they waited, ere their prayer
Brought answer through the silent air,
Till, weary, worn and wasted grown,
Their flesh had shrunk to skin and bone,
Then slowly changed to pulseless stone."
The tired feet first ceased to move,
Each joint grown solid to its groove;
Thence to the knees the strange spell spread;
Thence to the thighs, the heart, the head;
Then, like a moon-lit mist across the plain,
Went forth their spirits from these haunts of pain.

Supremely blest, they roam the fields
    Where Peace and Love and Plenty greet
    The brave and true, and good men meet
The rich rewards that Virtue yields.

The happy Dead! Do they forget
Their kindred dear, who linger yet
Amidst the mingled love and strife,
The joys and ills of mortal life?
Do they forget, 'midst joys above,
The springs where first they drank of love:
And, *in forgetfulness, forsake*
The land where human heartstrings break?
Nay! they *who love* can *ne'er* forget:
Who loved us first, they love us yet!

Forevermore in sympathy
With never-changing constancy,
Lel-lu-la and her Men-no-wee,
Endowed with attributes divine
And bosomed in this mural shrine,
Now serve in Love's sweet ministry,—
Mute prophets of fidelity.

Hither, with every blooming year,
They come, fond lovers' vows to hear;
And keep them to their pledges true,
Life's brief or lengthened journey through.

So therefore come they here for flowers
To deck their bridal robes and bowers;   -
And pluck the buds as potent charms
To woo true-lovers to their arms;
Or, pledging love's integrity,
Thereby take oath of constancy.

NOTES.

NOTE I, PAGE 13.

"Have swept this valiant band away."

The legend of Stone Idol is treated as if of Riccaree origin. It is more likely that it dates from a much earlier period than the migration of the Riccarees from the neighborhood of their relatives, the Pawnees, to this locality; that it attaches to the rocks as a fable of very ancient times. Memorials of a race, which roamed the shores of the upper Missouri long before Assiniboin or Sioux, Mandan or Ariccaree, exist all through this country, in traces of ancient fortifications, tombs, weapons of war and chase, and household implements, bearing sketches of domestic scenes, martial deeds, and the hunt. *Gone!* all save these memorials. And those who followed them are *gone* likewise, only excepting the remnants of the relentless Sioux, who must also soon disappear. War and pestilence (notably the smallpox, introduced among them by the traders) have utterly extinguished the Mandans, and have destroyed entire bands of the Riccarees, and pushed the remnant to a point more than two hundred miles distant from these storied rocks, which mark their former neighborhood.

NOTE II, PAGE 13.

"Attested down the years unknown
By pictograph and rough-hewn stone."

The rocky tablets of Western creek and river bluffs bear innumerable pictographic records of Indian parleys, ambushes, victories and defeats. They are usually merely rude outlines in red, blue and yellow pigments, laid on the natural surfaces of the rocks. Here it is a hunting scene, in which the hero won his "manhood name," and the first feather for his plume. There it is a battle. The tribes and particular bands engaged are denoted by their dress and several totems, or family signs,— beaver, badger, fox, or what not. Certain dots or lines over a prostrate figure record "the killed" and the scalps taken. A sort of petticoat and other marks indicate the number of women slain or carried captive; and so on to the end of the record. In some places the outlines of figures have been rudely *chiseled* in the face of the rock. One schooled in Indian lore will read these primitive stone-paged histories with scarce ever a doubt as to the interpretation.

Note III, Page 17.

"The golden moons, that come again."

Some of the Western Indians poetically term the summer, months "the golden moons," and have a pretty superstition, that Indian Summer is caused by the spirits of these months, returning, after the stormy equinox and first siftings from the snow-clouds, to look upon the beautiful earth once more, with pensive regret, before taking their final departure.

Note IV, Page 19.

"With wild, fantastic trip and spring."

This is the character of male dancing among the aborigines, —a series of quick, short jumps and springs, interspersed with extravagant gestures and grimaces, either comical or intended for earnest pantomime, in which struggles with wild beasts, or martial combats in all their details, down to the act of scalping, are depicted with horrible distinctness. While the men dance the women look on and applaud the pantomime and the recitals of the heroic deeds of braves and warriors, made in the form of song or speech as the dancing proceeds.

NOTE V, PAGE 19.

"Or turtle sliding from its log.
Or loosened turfs that seek the tide
From crumbling. flood-washed river side."

No description can convey an adequate impression of the solemn silence of solitude on the broad expanses of the Mississippi or Missouri, in the days of the early *voyageurs.* Imagine a solitary *voyageur,*—his frail canoe abandoned to the noiseless sweep of the strong middle-current of this wide stretching river, down gliding between far-off shores of illimitable forests, with no living thing in sight, for hours, but the water-snake or turtle basking on some floating log. At such a time one hears the whispering ripple under the canoe, and even the beating of his own heart. Then the plash of flashing fins, leaping from the water in sport or frightened flight, or the single liquid tone of turtle dropping into the current, is a *startling* sound. In the flood season crumblings from the edges of the river banks are frequent, and often hundreds of tons of earth give way and plunge into the swollen, swirling tide with a mighty sound, told from bluff to bluff, and repeated far away in the bowels of the deep forests, in echoes of thunder. Lewis & Clarke's journal says: "At one point a part of the cliff nearly three quarters of a mile long and two hundred feet high had plunged into the river." Further on the same journal says: "Shortly after midnight our sleepers were startled with the cry that the sand island was sinking. They scarcely got away with their boats before a part of the bank fell in and the island had disappeared." The author has seen places on the Mississippi where farms of many acres have utterly vanished in a single season.

Note VI, Page 20.

"Were prudish dames ne'er disobeyed."

Indian mammas are presumed to do all the match-making, and courting is, theoretically, dispensed with. But, as innumerable legends and such observations as appear in subsequent notes prove, the theory is not entire master of the practice.

Note VII, Page 40.

"The wondering menials, mute with fright."

Many Indian tribes maintain a system of slavery or serfhood. Captives, and criminals of their own tribes, are put to menial service, as hewers of wood and drawers of water, for chiefs or their immediate captors.

Note VIII, Page 43.

"Enwrapt our homes in midnight flame."

The word "home" applied to any savage lodge seems a misnomer. Yet if domestic felicity makes "home," there are many instances of it among the aborigines; and if permanent dwellings enter into this idea, the Riccarees had these,— comfortable octagon-shaped and cone-like lodges, covered with earth, fixed in permanent villages, guarded by police. They were good tillers of the soil, raising corn and melons, beans and squashes, not only for their own use, but to barter with their nomadic neighbors, the Sioux and Assiniboins.

Note IX, Page 45.

"He stands condemned his spear to yield,
And toil his lifetime in the field."

The degrading of warriors and hunters to the condition of *serfs*, for violation of tribal regulations, is a common practice to this day.

NOTE X, PAGE 48.

"Adorned with painted birds and flowers,
With pictured fruits and vines and bowers."

The thoroughly bleached and finely finished skins used among the tribes of the Northwest for robes and coverings, are to the Indian artist what the canvas is to his civilized brother. There he displays his highest genius, and his designs and execution are often really remarkable; not unworthy a place in some of our Academies of Fine Arts. But if his patrons have no stately halls and palace walls on which to exhibit the triumphs of his brush and pencil, they do him the honor to carry them on their persons. The chiefs delight to secure the finest talent of their tribes to depict the exploits of their lives upon their robes. For several fine specimens of this kind the reader is referred to Plates 306 to 312, inclusive, in Catlin's "North American Indians," Vol. II.

NOTE XI, PAGE 50.

"Thy shell-decked couch forsake."

Borderings and other decorations of garments and bed coverings were formerly wrought with small shells, as now with shells and bead-work. Some of the designs are exquisite.

NOTE XII, PAGE 51.

"So sing the amorous youths."

Padré Domineck and other writers describe the youths as going through the villages of the upper Missouri, on moonlight nights, singing love-sonnets. In another place Padré Domineck says: "Sometimes the Indian lover plays on his flute and sings songs of his own composition before the family wigwam of his beloved. Facilities for courting are not wanting, for in the simple habits of savage life young people often meet, and have opportunities for knowing each other."

Note XIII, Page 51.

"Like wine the matrons blest prepare."

The simple juice of the grape, fresh from the cluster, is the nearest approach to wine made by the North American Indians. Some of these hold the superstition that at the entrance to the Happy Hunting Grounds stand sainted matrons, pressing the juice from luscious heaps of grapes, to regale those who are so happy as to reach that beatific life. When they see a purple hue in the air they exclaim, "The matrons are pressing the grapes!"

Note XIV, Page 62.

"Almighty Te-wa-roob-tch, Spirit True."

This is the Riccaree (or Ariccaree) name for the Supreme Ruler, called by the Algonquin tribes Gezsha Manitou.

Note XV, Page 65.

Often doth sculptor Nature form
Rocks into rugged shapes of men."

There are many rocks in different parts of this country which bear strong resemblance to the profile of the human figure, and these, generally, are regarded by the Indians as tutelary genii.

Note XVI, Page 66.

"Then slowly changed to pulseless stone."

Lewis & Clarke's version of this legend says: "After wandering together and having nothing but grapes to subsist on, they were at last converted into stone, which, beginning at the feet, gradually invaded the nobler parts," until these sacred metamorphoses remained in place of the translated lovers.

www.ingramcontent.com/pod-product-compliance
Lightning Source LLC
Chambersburg PA
CBHW030022030726
47499CB00008B/3077